Egyptian Mythology

Myths and Gods of Ancient Egypt

Table of Contents

Introduction v

Chapter 1: The World and its First Gods 1

Chapter 2: The Osiris Myth 15

Chapter 3: Ra's Journey Through
            the Underworld 28

Chapter 4: The Pyramids and
            the Final Judgment...............47

Chapter 5: Deities and Creatures 59

Conclusion 63

References 66

Introduction

B y far, the ancient Egyptian civilization is one of the most intriguing, exciting, and awe-inspiring civilizations to ever exist, and part of that is because of its old age. After all, it is the second oldest civilization in the world, merely 500 years younger than the Mesopotamian civilization, which originated in modern-day Iraq and the surrounding region.

Most fascinating about the ancient Egyptians is that they were natural-born storytellers, which shows not only in their myths and gods, but also in how they lived their lives. They invented a unique writing system unique containing over 1,000 signs, including ideograms and phonograms, but that isn't all. The ancient Egyptians managed to fill the walls of their temples, palaces, tombs, obelisks, and even houses with their history, their stories, and the details of how they lived. They immortalized their history on stone, papyrus, and clay.

As you will see in their myths and legends, they used nature and the natural occurrences around them as the core inspiration for everything they wrote. As for why they wrote what they wrote, one can only guess. It could have been an attempt to make sense of the nature around them, for religious and political purposes, or because of their indoctrinated belief that Pharaohs were the link between gods and humans. A theory also states that historical events inspired some myths, but regardless, the reasons don't take away from the greatness of the writings. In fact, they only embellish it.

The only drawback of such excessive documentation, if it can be considered a drawback, is that we are now left with many accounts dating back to various ages. These accounts also differ in several details, such as the names of the gods, the events themselves, and the descriptions of the deities and places. Not only that, but many of the most detailed accounts were found on broken tablets. This all adds up to the fact that what we know about the beliefs of the ancient Egyptians, the stories they told, and the languages they spoke, is still very limited.

On the one hand, it can be disheartening to know that, for all we know, we will never get a single uniform account that explains or tells the full story of Egyptian myths. On the other hand, there is a profound beauty in the variety of perspectives. Ultimately, the content of stories and myths says more about its writers than about anything else, and that is what you will get to experience in the following pages.

How did the ancient Egyptians see nature, the world, and themselves? That is what we will explore throughout this book.

Chapter 1:

The World and its First Gods

According to Egyptian Mythology, in the beginning, the world was one. A single mass of darkness and chaos. The world's lack of shape and definition was expressed in the form of the four pairs of primordial gods. The first pair, Nu (male) and Nunet (female), represented the primordial water that fused together with the sky and the earth. From their union, the three other pairs of gods came into existence. The second pair, Hehu (male) and Hehut (female) represented infinite time, though they are also believed to have represented the space between the sky and the earth.

The third pair, Kekui (male) and Kekuit (female) represented the fusion of darkness and light.

Kekui stood for the darkest hour before dawn, while Kekuit stood for the darkness right after sunset. This could suggest that the world was in a permanent transitional state from day to night and night to day. The fourth and final pair, Kerh (male) and Kerhet (female) - although known by many other names - represented the state of the three previous pairs of gods, which was inactivity.

Through the four pairs of gods and goddesses, a state of fusion existed between male and female, sky, earth, the atmosphere between them, light, and darkness, and all was inactive. In the primordial sea that fused everything, it was believed that chaos existed. Apophis (chaos), a great serpent, permanently swirled through the water that was Nu and Nunet.

That was the state of the world until the spirit of creation decided to set itself in motion, therefore creating himself. Atum, the aforementioned creator, rose from Nu, the primordial water, on a large mass of land called Benben. He then shaped the undefined mass of water into an egg and willed the sun into existence. On his command, the ruse rose over the horizon, and at that moment, Ma'at was created.

Atum is said to have conducted those acts of creation through Heka, which was associated with energy. Eventually, Heka was promoted to a deity with his own priests, temples, and rituals. As for Ma'at, she is the concept of order, balance, and harmony personified in a goddess with wings of ostrich feathers. She is also considered the daughter of Ra and is why the world evolved from a state of disorder to order. She also plays an essential role in the trial of the dead.

Over the years, the identity of the sun god Ra (depicted as a man with the head of a falcon) was blended with that of Atum. In older myths, Atum manifested himself in the sun and then proceeded to create life and the rest of the gods, though in the more recent historical accounts, Atum created Ra, then Ra continued the process of creation. Because of the many common traits between Atum and Ra, they are often regarded as one composite god, Atum-Ra.

The story continues when Ra (Atum-Ra), on the primeval hill upon which he stood, created Shu and Tefnut out of his loneliness. Ra spat out of his mouth and created Shu, the god of dryness and air. After that, Ra had union with his own hand and secreted Tefnut from his body. Tefnut, depicted as a woman with the head of a tiger, became the goddess of humidity and rain.

The two siblings carried out their job, defining the lining between the sky and the earth that was yet to exist. That said, they were gone for too long. Meanwhile, on the Benben, Ra was filled with anguish due to the absence of his children, so he took out his eye and sent it in search for them, hence the Eye of Ra. Eventually, Shu and Tefnut returned and with them their father's eye. Once he was reunited with his children, Ra wept with tears of joy and as his heavy tears landed on the Benben below, creating humankind, men, and women.

Seeing as Ra's creation had no place to live, and the Benben was not enough to house them all, Tefnut and Shu mated to bring to life Geb and Nut. Geb, the god of the earth (often seen with the head of the Nile goose and a snake around his neck) and Nut, the goddess of the sky, symbolized by a water pot over her head. With the creation of Shu,

Tefnut, Geb, and Nut, the four basic terrains were created: Air, Water, Earth, and Sky.

Geb and Nut, despite being siblings, fell in a love so powerful, yet Ra didn't approve of their actions. Because he couldn't keep them from each other, he decided to separate them forcefully. The infuriated Ra ordered Shu to create a space between Geb and Nut so that they may forever see each other but never get to touch. Nevertheless, it was already too late since Nut was pregnant with Geb's seed. So, as the earth and sky parted, the sky, Nut, gave birth.

From the mating of Geb and Nut, four other gods came to being, two sons and two daughters. Set, the god with a dog-like face, was known as the god of war, destruction, and disorder. His brother, Osiris, was the god of life, fertility, and agriculture. Later on, Osiris became the god of the afterlife, the dead, and the judge of the underworld. He was depicted as a green-skinned man and was seen by the ancient Egyptians as the bringer of life.

As for the daughters, there was Nephthys who represented death and Isis who represented life.

While Nephthys was Set's partner, Isis was Osiris,' and she played a major role in Osiris and Set's animosity. With this birth of Set, Nephthys, Osiris, and Isis, the principles of life and death were set in motion.

Ra's Rule

When the humans were created, and for them, the earth they started populating, Ra's rule extended to them. At first, life went on as usual with the gods living among their people in Heliopolis, which translates to the city of the sun – but things changed as Ra grew older and less fit for rule.

One myth says that due to her rebellious nature, Isis sought the control and power that belonged to the mighty god, Ra. The goddess was already of infinite wisdom and almost god-like in knowledge. Nevertheless, she lacked the power of the great creator, so she made it her goal to acquire his power through the one way she could, namely, by knowing his secret name.

In Egyptian mythology, a god's secret name was what gave them their power and their abilities.

Each god's secret name was meant to be known only to them since, once a god's name is revealed, their power could be used against them.

With the desire for power in her heart, Isis decided to visit Ra, where his double throne (symbolic of the northern and southern kingdoms) was erected. As the old god walked, a little spittle fell from his mouth and onto the earth, next to Isis's feet. The goddess saw it was a perfect opportunity, took his spittle along with a handful of the fertile earth, and shaped the mixture into a serpent. She then laid it down in Ra's usual passage that took him to his kingdoms.

Unaware, as Ra stepped down the road, the sacred serpent came to life and sunk its poisoned fangs into the god's flesh. With a mighty cry that penetrated the skies above, life began to drain out of Ra's body. His sons with him leaped to rescue his collapsing body, and though he tried to explain, he could not speak.

The poison rushed to his veins, causing him great agony, the source of which he didn't know - it was a life that was not created by him so he couldn't command it. Isis then came up to Ra, feigning concern for the dying god. She told him it was a snake that chose to rebel against its own creator and poison him. Being the goddess of life, her words bore with them a great power known and felt by Ra. Isis knew that in his hour of need and torment, Ra was desperate enough and willing to speak his name onto her.

Isis offered to cure him, but she insisted he give her his name in return. As the pain got stronger, Ra finally conceded and gave his consent for Isis to search within him, and by doing so, he forfeited his name, letting it pass onto Isis. Having succeeded in becoming the mistress of the gods, Isis commanded the poison to leave Ra's body and spare his life.

The Rebellion and Separation of Mankind

The story of how the world of humans was separated from the world of the gods began with men rebelling against Ra. It all took place when the humans realized that their creator, Ra, was too old and worn with age. When men realized that, they started conspiring against him, but because Ra was all-knowing, their words and schemes didn't go by unnoticed. Ra had no mercy to offer his betrayers, and though he was filled with great sadness, he called for all the gods to meet with him on the Benben.

Shu, Tefnut, Geb, Nut, and all the other gods and forces which he created came to him, bowed, and waited for his words. Despite his wrath, Ra decided not to take his revenge until Nu, whom he considered his ancestor, had given him further instructions. So, Ra cried out to his ancestor for guidance, and according to the Egyptologist Sir Wallis Budge, Nu answered:

"Thou art the god who art greater than he that made thee, and who art the sovereign of those who were created by him, thy throne is set, and the fear of thee is great; let then thine Eye be upon those who have uttered blasphemies against thee" (Budge, 1904, p.364).

Nu had instructed Ra to send his eye to seek revenge on mankind, and the god obeyed. The rest of the gods watched as the race of man fled to the mountains. Ra had instructed Hathor, his feminine counterpart, to come down on mankind in the form of the goddess Sekhmet, a ferocious and vengeful lioness. Sekhmet brought down Ra's fury on humanity, and it was said that by the end of her first attack, she had been wading in the blood of her victims.

Regretting his decision, Ra decided to summon back Sekhmet and call her off, but a thirst for revenge overcame her. Sekhmet ran wild, killing and slaughtering whoever crossed her sights. Horror filled Ra as he realized that humanity might come to an end at the hands of Sekhmet.

The sun god then called upon his fastest messengers and ordered them to go to Elephantine – an island on the Nile – and gather as many mandrakes as they could. When they did, Ra ordered them to send the mandrakes to Heliopolis, where the women crushed the barley to make beer. There, the mandrakes were crushed all the same and added to the beer. They made seven thousand vessels of beer made of slaughtered men's blood and crushed mandrake.

All the while, Sekhmet was still on her rampage, making her way along the Nile. The only way Ra could protect humankind was to trick her. So, during the night while the people were asleep, the god ordered the seven thousand vessels be spilled on a piece of land until it was covered in the blood-red mixture, and the messengers obeyed. In the morning, Sekhmet had arrived at the land, looking for men to kill, but all she found was blood; the lioness rejoiced in the fact that they were already dead.

In celebration, Sekhmet drank from the blood-red mixture until she had had her heart's content, but the beer mixed with mandrake had made her drunk and docile. When she lost sight of her goal to annihilate mankind, Ra called her to him, and she obeyed, after which Ra had managed to preserve what was left of humanity.

When Sekhmet had reverted to Hathor and was by Ra's side again, along with the rest of the gods, Ra let his thoughts be known. He felt deep regret for the ungodly violence he had brought on them. At the same time, he was tired of mankind. Even though he had killed many, and to him, the rest were without value, he could not bring himself to kill them because the act was beneath him.

The myth suggests that Ra then went and expressed his weariness to Nu, who responded by transferring the burden of ruling to Ra's son, Shu. After that, Nu ordered Nut, the sky goddess, to assume her cow form and carry Ra to his kingdom in the sky, away from mankind.

As Ra's worshippers on earth watched their god leave, they were filled with regret and a desire to avenge him. After arming themselves, those dedicated to Ra made their way to the territories of Ra's betrayers. From the back of Nut, Ra watched his worshippers avenge him, and for that, he decided to build them a field in his kingdom called the field of Hetep. It was the heavenly paradise where the pure souls went after passing through the dangers of the underworld and the final trial.

Ra's Journey

The sun god was believed to be on a permanent journey between the underworld and the surface. In ancient times, this explained mornings, nights, sunrises, and sunsets. Aboard his celestial boat, Ra, along with his company of gods and the dead pharaohs, would sail across the sky each morning, bringing light and life to the Egyptians. Meanwhile, the great serpent Apophis, the primordial god of chaos and disorder, waited, trapped in the underworld, unable to give chase.

Apophis had always resided within the primordial waters and thrived in the chaos since before creation. However, Ra's order brought to the world a force that opposed Apophis' very existence, which enraged the malicious serpent. So, each night, the indestructible Apophis attempted to put an end to Ra and his rule. During eclipses and cloudy days, the ancient Egyptians believed that Apophis was succeeding in defeating Ra and the gods and stopping the sun's journey across the sky. Nevertheless, the morning sky was never a place of battle.

The real battle between Ra and Apophis occurred every night, as Ra's boat disappeared from the sky and entered the underworld, the domain of Apophis, and many other demons. At the gates of the underworld, Apophis waited. One account mentions that as the sun god's solar boat neared the gates of the underworld, Apophis rose and, with his eyes, hypnotized all those on the boat except for Set, the son of Geb and Nut, and the god of destruction and war.

Set then endorsed the role of protecting Ra by fending off the serpent with his spear until they were far enough from Apophis. After that, the journey through the underworld continued, and the sun was made to shine again. Other accounts state that Ra took on the form of a giant cat and dismembered Apophis. In these telling's, the serpent regenerated every night and returned to attack Ra's boat. The ancient Egyptians believed that they had to help their gods pass safely through the underworld, and so they used to build wax figures of the snake which they then spat on, disfigured, and dismembered. They believed the action would give the gods an advantage against Apophis.

Chapter 2:

The Osiris Myth

It was said that Osiris, son of Geb and Nut, brother to Set, Nephthys, and Isis, was one of the greatest rulers in ancient Egypt. Because he was the god of fertility, agriculture, and life, the reign of Osiris reign was a time of peace and prosperity for the Egyptians. He had taught them the precepts of agriculture, blessed their lands, and maintained peace and order within the kingdom for the longest time. He also married his sister, Isis, the powerful deity who possessed a great deal of knowledge and the ability to create life, use magic, and heal. Not to mention, she was able to trick the great god Ra himself.

The powerful pair Osiris and Isis ruled over Egypt, guaranteeing a happy life for all their subjects, until one day when Set decided it was time for a change. When it came to Set's motive for killing his brother, Osiris, there is no one clear motive. Some accounts mention that it was because Set was the god of war, destruction, and disorder, and the fact that Osiris had great power and was able to keep a peaceful rule ignited Set's jealousy.

Other versions of the myth claim it was out of spite because Osiris had laid with Set's sister and wife, Nephthys. However, Plutarch added that it was Nephthys who seduced Osiris by disguising herself as Isis, and so he had relations with her (Plutarch & Fowler, 1936, p.39). As a result, Nephthys was pregnant with Anubis, the jackal-headed god of death and tombs' protector.

Regardless of the underlying motive, Set's jealousy led him to plot the murder of his older brother. After taking Osiris' exact measurements one time while he was asleep, Set built a magnificent coffin to perfectly fit his brother. Then, at a party that Set had organized, he presented his coffin and announced to the guests that whoever fits inside the coffin could have it to themselves. When it was Osiris' turn, and he had gone inside the coffin, Set locked the coffin, trapping him inside.

The coffin was quickly taken to the Nile and thrown into the depths, and with that, Set had gotten rid of his brother, or at least he thought he did. When Isis heard of her husband's murder, she was overcome by grief, but she knew she had to find the coffin in which he was imprisoned. Plutarch's version of the story mentions that the river Nile had carried the coffin along its length and to the Mediterranean Sea.

There, the coffin managed to stay afloat until it ended up on the shores of Byblos, a city in Phoenicia, now known as Lebanon. In Byblos, the coffin lodged itself in what was believed to be either a tamarisk tree or a cedar. The tree then grew around the coffin, trapping Osiris inside. The only evidence of an unusual occurrence was that the tree exuded a particularly sweet smell.

Malcander, the king of Phoenicia at the time, along with his wife Astarte, found the tree, and enamored by its sweet smell, ordered it to be cut and used as an ornamental pillar in their palace. Meanwhile, Isis and Nephthys, in their kite forms (bird of prey) had been looking all over for their brother, in vain. Then Isis was informed that the coffin had washed up on the shores of Byblos. She went to the city disguised as an old lady, and when she had reached the coastal city, she sat weeping on the shore. There, the queen's maidens approached her and spoke with her. She didn't reveal her identity, but one of her characteristics as a goddess was her beautiful fragrance steeped in the maidens' garments.

When the maidens returned to the palace, the queen noticed the fragrance that surrounded them and inquired about it. Without hesitation, they referred their mistress to Isis, the goddess in disguise. The queen took an interest in Isis and hired her as a nurse for her son. While the goddess accepted the position, she attempted to nurse the queen's child with her fire, making him immortal. When the queen discovered this, she was furious, and that was when Isis revealed her true nature.

She revealed herself as the great Egyptian goddess, and the king and queen's immediate response was to bow at her feet and see to her need. Isis had only one demand, namely the ornamental wooden pillar where Osiris' coffin was lodged. Upon their swift agreement, Isis took an ax to the pillar and managed to free her husband's coffin from the pillar's core. But bad news awaited her.

Too much time had passed, and her brother-husband was dead inside. The goddess wept, but she didn't hesitate to find another solution. Eventually, she decided it was best to take Osiris's body back to Egypt. There, she could gather the knowledge and ingredients needed for her to resurrect him from the dead, but the only thing that stood in her way was Set. Isis needed to keep the body hidden from Set, and that was why she hid the body in the Nile Delta under Nephthys' protection.

Nephthys relationship with Set was quite troubled. Though he was her husband and brother, he managed to make her fear him greatly. When Set suspected that something was awry, it didn't take him long to extract the truth out of Nephthys, and that was how he knew Osiris's body was not gone. Fearing that Isis might succeed, Set wasted no time finding the body where it was kept, and once he did, he dismembered Osiris's corpse, cutting him into fourteen pieces.

To ensure that the body was never reassembled, Osiris flung the pieces all over Egypt to make sure that it could never again be put together. When Isis had returned, she found that the body was gone and grieved yet another time before she rallied her sister to help her locate Osiris's remains. Together, the sisters traveled all over Egypt, gathering Osiris's body parts piece by piece.

By the time they were done, Isis had assembled all of his body, except for his penis, which she could not retrieve. It had been thrown in the Nile and eaten by a species of elephant fish called medjed. Without his penis, Osiris was incomplete, which meant he couldn't stay alive, even if he were resurrected. However, this didn't keep Isis from trying. She called upon Thoth, the god of wisdom, science, and magic, who revealed to her the resurrection spell she needed to utter. Anubis, the god of death, mummification, and embalming, also helped Isis restore and embalm Osiris's body.

Thanks to her powers, Isis was able to resurrect Osiris's body for long enough so she could turn to her kite form and have sexual intercourse with him. Whether his genitalia was reconstructed through magic or Isis managed to extract his seed, the accounts differ. Still, the outcome of Isis bearing a child is always the same. Their intercourse results in Isis getting pregnant with Horus.

As for Osiris, because he was incomplete, he was unable to live and rule over the surface world. Instead, he was forced to retire to the underworld, where he presided as judge and ruler over the domain and all who entered. That is how he became a god responsible for the matters of the dead and the afterlife.

Horus's Revenge

While Set ruled over Egypt with an iron fist, spreading terror, droughts, and his heart's content of malice, the pregnant Isis laid in hiding. She was frightened of what would happen to her if Set were to find out she was still alive, and not only that, but also pregnant with Osiris's offspring. In the Delta region, the goddess lasted throughout her pregnancy, and long after that while she took care of her son, Horus.

Nevertheless, Isis was not alone. She used to hide during the day and come out at night to gather the growing Horus's food. Serket, the goddess of nature, medicine, and the healing of stings, protected her by sending seven scorpions to keep her safe. Other gods also helped her by protecting Horus while Isis left to get what she and her son needed to survive.

As her son grew in strength and might, Isis began telling him of his uncle, Set, and how his father, Osiris, was betrayed and murdered by him. As Horus developed an understanding of his place in the kingdom and the reality of his father's murder, he grew vengeful and eager to reclaim what was rightfully his. When Horus, the falcon-headed god of the sky, became powerful enough, he left his mother and went to stand before the great nine; Atum-Ra, Shu, Tefnut, Geb, Nut, Isis, Osiris, Nephthys, and Set.

The young god made his case, arguing that he was the rightful heir to the throne and that Set was nothing but a spiteful usurper. Since the truth was known to all, the majority of votes went towards returning the throne back to his rightful heir. It was only because of Ra's vote that the odds turned to Set's favor. The creator god Ra refused to give the throne to Horus because of his young age. He favored Set's experience and wisdom over Horus's droll courage and naivete.

With the council at odds, Isis took matters into her own hand. She disguised herself as a pretty woman, frail and in distress. She took her act to the steps of Set's palace. Seeing the weeping woman, Set ran to her aid. When he asked her what was wrong, she said that her husband had died and that a stranger had assumed ownership over their livestock. When her son had asked for the cattle, the man threatened to have the boy killed.

Without hesitation, Set condemned the stranger's actions and assured her that he would help her and her son take back what was rightfully theirs. Once he spoke his answer, Isis revealed her original form, mocked her brother, and took to the sky in her falcon form, announcing Set's decision to the gods.

Nevertheless, the relentless Set insisted on challenging Horus. The rules were those who were able to establish dominance over the other, winning Egypt's throne. The battle, however, was not an easy feat. In fact, their series of challenges lasted for 80 years.

One of their first challenges was proposed by Set and consisted of a simple breath-holding contest. The two gods were to turn to hippopotami and dive into the Nile. The loser was the first to cave in and come back to the surface for air. After a long time had passed, Isis grew anxious for her son since she desperately wanted him to take the throne. Overcome by anxiety and desire, Isis fashioned a harpoon and flung it into the water. To her misfortune, the tip of the weapon found its way into Horus's flesh. Pain coursed through the young god, but he remained submerged. Isis then freed the harpoon from her son and took another shot at her brother. This time, it worked. The harpoon sank deep into Set's flesh, and the pain was almost too much to bear.

On the verge of losing, Set pled and appealed to his sister's sentimental side. Under pressure, Isis collapsed, and she healed her brother's wound. The act infuriated Horus, who leaped out of the water, turned to his original form, decapitated his mother with one swift strike and walked away.

As Horus walked off, leaving Set and Isis behind, Ra reunited Isis's head with her body. The young god strayed on foot until he found a tree, which he laid under. Set, who had been following Horus from a distance, decided to attack once Horus was asleep. The time quickly came, and Set assaulted Horus, gouging his eyes out before leaving him where he was.

Because of her benevolence and pity, the goddess Hathor took on the young eyeless god and decided to make him a new set of eyes. For that, she filled his eye sockets with sacred milk, thereby healing his wounds and giving him new eyes. Horus was furious at Set, but under pressure from the council of gods, the two contenders were ordered to make peace and carry on with the challenges.

Set was not one for following rules. Rather than abide by the challenges, he opted to establish dominance over Horus using any means necessary. So, one day, while Horus slept, Set forced himself into the unconscious young god. However, Horus woke up just in time and managed to catch Set's semen in his hands, defeating Set's attempt to dominate Horus. To avenge himself, Horus went to his mother for help, and in turn, she went to Set's farmers. When she asked about Set's vegetable of choice, the farmer said it was lettuce. Upon discovering this piece of information, Horus spread his semen on a lettuce leaf to establish his dominance over his uncle.

When Set stood before the council of gods the second time, believing he had put his seed in Horus, he demanded the throne be awarded to him. At which point Horus objected and demanded that Thoth calls upon both of the gods' semen on the grounds of Set's untruthfulness. The council agreed, and Thoth called upon the gods' semen. Set's semen answered from the Nile, where Horus' hands were cleansed. Horus's answered from Set's stomach, where it was swallowed along with the lettuce leaves.

To Horus's misfortune, Set managed to convince the council to arrange yet another challenge despite him losing based on his own terms. The council of gods willed that the ultimate challenge is a boat race across the Nile, to the exception that the boats were to be made of stone. Set made his own boat out of stone, and it immediately sank. Horus, by contrast, was a tad more clever. He made his boat out of wood but covered it in plaster, which gave the boat's hull the appearance of the stone. With ease, he sailed on the Nile until the infuriated Set turned into a hippopotamus and smashed through Horus's boat. Needless to say, the challenge's results were not taken into consideration on account of Horus's cheating.

After nearly 80 years of wait, the council decided that the matter had taken too long. At last, they deferred to Osiris's judgment since he was the former king, and he had the right to choose. So, the council sent for the ruler of the underworld, who chose Horus as the rightful heir to the throne. Osiris also insisted that Set be punished for his actions. Some accounts say that Set was banished, whereas others claim that the land was divided between both. However, the most common resolution is where Horus won, and that Set was punished in some form or another.

Chapter 3:

Ra's Journey Through the Underworld

As apparent from their writings, the ancient Egyptians believed in the existence of souls. Even more perceptible in their scriptures and their way of life was their concrete belief in the afterlife. This spanned from their magnificent tombs to their religious texts, gods, and most importantly, their expertise in mummification and the techniques of body preservation. The concept of life after death played a determining role in the life of the average Egyptian.

General Description of the Underworld

The realm of the dead, also known as 'Duat,' is where Egyptians believed the dead went after leaving the surface world. The underworld has a great significance in almost all Egyptian myths since Osiris presides over it. It is also where many demons and creatures live, including the great serpent Apophis. Not to mention, the underworld is where Ra's solar ship passes to get to the other side and rise again as a new sun.

In itself, it is not a place of punishment or reward, but a way of the station. Despite being the domain of many demons, beasts, and foul creatures, the underworld is simply an area that the dead had to cross to stand before the assessors of Ma'at, who judged each soul. There, the final weighing of the heart decided whether the person got the punishment or the reward. The underworld is divided into twelve regions, one for each hour that the sun (Ra's solar ship) spent away from the sky.

One of the texts that provided the most details as to what awaited the dead when they arrived in the underworld was the Book of the Dead. It was a scroll with a collection of spells and instructions, usually written by a priest or a scribe under the instruction of those who could afford such a privilege. The book of the dead was an instruction manual on how to survive the underworld and reach the afterlife.

Interestingly, while the collective books of the dead shared many similarities, they did share many differences as well. The most fundamental difference is that each book of the dead was tailored to the person who commissioned it. Each person required a certain set of spells to make their way to the other side. That meant each book of the dead differed in length, content, and it was all influenced by the underworld's common view at the time.

The Duat was a place engulfed in deep darkness and separated from the surface world by a range of mountains. There was a valley within those mountains, and through the valley flowed a river, much like the river Nile. Many creatures and beings lived on either side of that river. This circular valley full of horrors was the Duat, which, throughout the many inscriptions, was cemented as an abysmal, frightening dead land.

The First Hour

As established, the underworld was divided into twelve sections, each one representing an hour of the night. The Egyptians believed that a dead soul's journey started out when Ra entered the realm at sundown. This is what is said about the first region of the underworld.

To reach the other world, the great Ra is said to enter a hall where his form changes to fit the world of the dead. Inside the hall, he is awaited by apes who open the doors to him, granting him entrance. As he sails through, the apes guide his boat, singing his praises and hymns until he has entered the underworld. In the hall, aside from the apes, one can find the trapped souls of the dead as well as several gods, though the gods are unspecified.

As for the souls of the dead, these belonged to the people who were unqualified to enter the realm of the dead. According to ancient Egyptian religious customs, several funerary ceremonies and rites had to take place to prepare the soul for the underworld. Nevertheless, not all could afford these expensive rituals. Consequently, many souls ended up trapped inside the hall, neutral ground between both worlds.

As he sails his boat, Ra is escorted by a company of gods - the same company that traveled with him across the skies in the morning. The one new addition to the boat, however, was a guide who changed every hour. Each region had a specific guide and patron who boarded the boat to aid their supreme god through to the realm of the dead.

The Second Hour

Ra's solar boat sails across the river until it reaches the second gate of the underworld, guarded by the gods known as the Souls of the Duat. For a human soul to cross those gates, they had to know each god by their secret name. If the human soul, when on earth, had prayed to the Souls of the Duat and offered sacrifices, that soul would be granted the gods' favor and an advantage over the other human souls.

As the gods of the Duat witness their supreme god Ra's passing, they speak to him, offering him their praises. On Ra's command, the Souls of the Duat tend to the passing souls of the dead by granting them sustenance, water, and by making them whole again in cases of dismemberment. It is also said that the words the Souls of the Duat spoke to Ra could help a soul during its journey if the soul could understand the words.

Osiris, the lord of the second hour, rules over with the Souls of the Duat by his side. As Ra's boat makes its way, it is guided forward by four boats ahead of it. First, there is Osiris' boat, then Isis's boat, then the third boat of a god believed to be Wepwawet, the one who opens ways. Fourth, there is the boat of Nepr, who was considered another aspect or another manifestation of Osiris. There is a combined total of forty-two gods and goddesses on either side of the four boats, twenty-one on each side.

Inside the second gate, there were gods, but there were also enemies. Most notably, there was Apophis, the great serpent who was eventually conquered by Ra, Set, and the rest of Ra's company. Other enemies do attempt to prevent the god's passage, but Osiris' followers thwart them; these are souls who pledged unwavering servitude to Osiris on earth and were destined to protect Ra in his travels.

The Third Hour

As with the previous gate, to cross the third gate, a human soul must know the gods' secret names who preside over this third region of the underworld, known as the 'Hidden Souls.' Knowing the names meant that the human soul could not only pass unharmed, but it would also be rewarded with abundant water for its field in the afterlife.

Similar to the Souls of the Duat, offering sacrifices for the Hidden Souls guaranteed the passing souls a significant upper hand. However, should the passing soul fail to name the gods, they were to fall into the gods' cauldrons. Collectively, the Hidden Souls were more terrifying than the Souls of the Duat. They were originally created and called upon by Ra to protect Osiris and keep him safe, which explains why they were armed with fiery cauldrons and screamed terror-inducing roars.

Ahead of Ra, there are three boats, and on those boats were several forms of the god Osiris who guided Ra through the third hour. While he sails through, Ra calls upon the Hidden Souls to protect Osiris. He blesses them for their protection of his own self, reminds them of the physical bodies and the estates he has already given them, and the rewards that awaited them. With that, he leaves the region and passes into the fourth hour.

The Fourth Hour

By the fourth region, the treacherous nature of the underworld begins to expose itself. While most of the proceedings were ceremonial and filled with blessings and praises in the previous one, this region is one of the first that harbors many enemies. Here, the enemies are hordes of snakes so vicious that even Ra commands protection from his followers and companions against the dangers.

In order to gain access to the territory, a human soul must once again know the secret names of the invisible gods that reign over the region. Only then can it enter the fourth region, see the invisible guides, and survive all of its dangers and monsters.

Instead of sailing through the river as he normally would, the danger force Ra to travel through the terrain in a different manner. His solar boat is said to transform into a massive two-headed serpent that spits fire from its mouths. For protection, the ship is led into narrow passages made of sand and pulled across the terrain by his company of gods and servants, and even then, the procession still witnesses many monsters and creatures.

Through the palpable darkness, the first snake that comes into passing rides a boat featuring two human heads, one on each end. The second snake has two wings, three heads, and four human legs upon which it walks. Third, a two-headed snake with yet another snake head in place of its tail. In addition, more snakes come along the way, and they vary in the number of heads - some of them also feature human heads.

In the end, Ra's procession passes by a giant scorpion and the goddess Uraeus, who takes on the form of a massive cobra. After passing the last snakes, they approach the gates of the fifth section.

The Fifth Hour

The fifth region is where Ra is pulled by his company of gods across a great capital city's roads.

For a human to gain entrance, they must know the names of the hidden gods, and in reward, their souls are granted eternal peace and satisfaction. The reward is said to increase in value depending on whether the human devoted enough sacrifices for the hidden gods and Seker, the falcon-headed lord of the fifth region.

During Ra's journey in this domain, he passes upon a small hill on which lies a human head with a scarab for a face. That is said to represent Khepri, who, in turn, represents renewal. The scarab is a sign of the hidden cave where Seker resides. As such, Ra's procession takes the path under the scarab-head and into the sand cavern, which is guarded by two sphinxes and two snakes.

After passing the sphinx, Ra is met with Seker, riding on a massive, winged snake with two heads. In Seker's domain, there is also a lake of water, but rather than having water-like qualities, it only possessed the appearance of a liquid. Only those in the lake got to experience the true reality of the lake, namely fire, whose scorching heat was used as a means of punishing those who the gods had deemed evil.

Ra's serpent boat then moves past the lake and finds a sealed chamber full of sand and watched by a two-headed serpent. Several texts mention that this sand chamber contains the very seed of life itself. There is a final assembly of seven gods past the chamber who exact their vengeance on the people who have earned it. Those who angered the gods are condemned to be killed at the hands of those gods each day, as Ra passes through the underworld.

The Sixth Hour

In this region, Ra's serpent-shaped vessel returns to its original form, the solar boat on which he travels the skies. The sixth domain is where Ra makes his way back to the water, where Toth and the goddess Ament-semu-set lead him. To be granted entrance, one must know the names of the guardians of the gate. However, to pass safely to the seventh hour, they must also be able to remain focused and resist the goddess's attempts of distraction.

Within the domain, there is a house with sixteen divisions occupied by gods and spirits employed to guard the five-headed snake. Inside the massive, twisted body of the snake lies a man on his back. His head is that of a scarab, symbolizing Kheperi's death. It is believed to signify resurrection because as Ra speaks his words of life, the god's body starts moving.

What comes after the serpent are the three shrines of Ra, all guarded by serpent gods. They are said to represent his three forms (body, mind, and soul) since the symbols on the shrines are a lion (physical strength), a human head (consciousness), and a wing (signifier of spirit).

On the shore to Ra's left, there is yet another gigantic serpent, although that one is tasked with devouring Ra's enemies, whether they are spirits, demons, or shadows. The serpent protects him during his passing through what is believed to be the primordial waters of Nu.

The Seventh Hour

The gate of this region is known as the 'Gate of Osiris.' It bears this name because it is where Osiris chose to build his abode, away from the sights of Apophis, the primordial serpent, and the enemies of Ra and Him. The abode, blessed by Isis's powers, bestows the solar boat with a type of magic that enables it to hover over the land where there is no river.

While Apophis is under the spell of the hidden abode, unaware of his surroundings, Ra strikes the great serpent with his knife. This explains the several accounts that portray Ra as a cat slaying Apophis the serpent. In many religious scriptures, it is also referenced that many blessings are promised for the souls that create statues for the serpent and recreate its death at the hands of the great god.

Several books of the dead contain Isis' spells and utterances, which are recited by the dead to weaken Apophis. Those souls who aid in the killing of the snake are promised a high position alongside Ra.

On some of Ra's journeys, Apophis is said to become strong enough that he remains undefeated. In those times, Isis, Set, the goddess Serkhet, along with Her-tesu-f and four of Osiris' female manifestations, bind the serpent in chains and stab it with their weapons until Ra has safely made it through.

The Eighth Hour

What characterizes and makes the eighth domain so unique is its circles. While there is not much information about any resemblance to the real-life of ancient Egyptians, the circles, the doors, and what is kept behind each door is quite intriguing.

As the gods of the eighth region pull ra's boat, he passes several circles with doors. The door to each circle holds behind it either gods or monsters. To each, Ra calls, and they reply, though never in their true voices, but in the voices of many things, from weeping women to moaning men and tortured beings. Eventually, Ra reaches the end of the domain after passing the circles.

The Ninth Hour

When Ra arrives in the ninth region, he speaks to the gods standing on the shores. He declares that whoever knows the names of the gods shall be rewarded with a place of authority in the underworld. As Ra sails, he is preceded with what is believed to be small baskets carrying twelve godly rowers, whose secondary duty is to throw Ra's blessed water on the spirits that stand watch on the shores. However, the main duty of the rowers is to guide Ra to the place where he can resurrect the sun.

On either side of Ra, spirits and creatures are watching. To his right, there are twelve gods and goddesses whose words of life empower Osiris. To Ra's left, there are twelve uraei, which are cobra snakes that breathe fire in acknowledgment of their god. At this point, Ra is close to reaching the end of his journey.

The Tenth Hour

Ra's scepter turns into a snake when he enters the tenth domain of the underworld. The snake is said to have two heads, one wearing a red crown and the other a white crown. Each color represented one half of his kingdom, namely the north-south. The snake also had four human legs, two for each head. The snake was curved, and a black hawk (Horus) was standing in the curvature of its body.

Then, a procession of fully armed serpents and gods makes its way towards Ra. They follow the god as he sails towards the east, and they put down all his enemies while he safely crosses the region. However, Ra witnesses a few interesting scenes on his way out, the first of which is a living scarab beetle.

Further down the domain, he sees two snakes supporting a round disk with their necks. He sails a little further and sees a group of goddesses being given the Eye of Horus to care for it. Ra also sees eight more gods on their way to vanquish his enemies, twelve aquatic beings, and four goddesses, each with a serpent head growing out of its back. Finally, on his way out of the region, he finds Set, the lord of the domain who stands up and travels with him to the next domains.

The Eleventh Hour

Ra's scepter returns to its original form, and on his ship appears a large solar disk encircled by a snake. The disk's purpose is to show Ra the way through the pitch-black darkness of the under-world. As he sails on, he is preceded by snakes and gods, including the four forms of Neith, the goddess of war, and one of the manifestations of Nunet, the female counterpart of Nu, the primor-dial water.

This instance is believed to symbolize the sun ris-ing over the sea. Ra then continues through the passage, which is of both the utmost beauty and terror. He first meets a god with three heads, one being a solar disk and the two sprouting from it being human heads. This god is said to be one of those at Ra's side until sunrise, but he never leaves the underworld. As the god sails through the un-derworld, he is met with another procession of serpent gods, multi-headed beings, and goddesses riding on uraei.

To Ra's left side, he sees the burning city of the eleventh hour where Horus and his ser-pent-headed weapon are vanquishing the ene-mies of Ra. Outside the city lurks a giant ser-pent, said to be as old as a million years, wait-ing for those who somehow manage to escape Horus's offensive. In front of the city were five pits, designed for torturing Ra's enemies, with each being under the command of a god or a goddess. By destroying the five fragments of the soul, the purpose of the pits was to ensure there would be no chance of future existence for those transgressors.

The first pit had the enemies picking their heads with axes while a lion goddess spewed them with fire before cutting them to pieces. The second teemed with dead bodies under the command of another fire-spitting goddess who also cut her victims with a monstrous blade. The third pit was dedicated to torturing the enemies' souls in the same manner as the other two pits, with divine fire and knives. The fourth contained the enemies' shadows, one of the fragments of the soul in ancient Egyptian beliefs. The fifth housed their heads, and both chambers were lit on fire.

In the end, Ra passes along a valley where he is met with four enemies standing on their heads. Ra commands Osiris to cut them down, then looks to his enemies and details the tortures that await them in the five infernal pits.

The Twelfth Hour

At last, this is the hour of rebirth for Ra. Once he enters the twelfth and final domain, he is born again, and when this occurs, the primordial gods of water and time, Nu, Nut, Heh, and Hehut, enter the city to carry Ra back to the surface world. There, the god with a solar disk for a head turns into a dung beetle, a symbol often associated with the rising sun.

Ra's boat is then pulled through the body of a serpent where he emerges from the mouth into the surface world. Once the journey has been complete, a new life and a new day are born, and the blessings of Ra are distributed over his company of gods and the helpful souls he encountered on his perilous journey.

Chapter 4:

The Pyramids and the Final Judgment

It is common knowledge that there are three great pyramids in Egypt. A lesser-known piece of information is that these three are not the only ones in the country; the total figure exceeds one hundred pyramids, and these are only the discovered ones to date. While those three iconic pyramids, Khufu, Khefre, and Menkaure, are the largest and the most unaffected by time structure-wise, many Egyptians made sure to build themselves a fitting tomb for the afterlife. Now, to understand the significance of the pyramids, one must deepen their understanding of what happens to the soul after death, aside from journeying through the underworld.

The Final Judgment

When a human dies, their soul is escorted by Anubis to the doors of the Hall of Ma'at, also known as the 'Hall of the Two Truths.' This is where their trial takes place to determine whether they will go to the Field of Reeds and receive eternal blessings or if they will die a second, permanent death. A person's book of the dead prepared them for their trial in front of Ma'at in her two forms, her forty-two judges known as the assessors of Ma'at, and the gods present.

At the sacred doors of the Hall of Ma'at, the dead were only granted entrance if they were able to name each door panel accurately. Once they were able to do so, they were led to stand in line along with the rest of the souls awaiting judgment. When it was their turn to be judged, the dead walked to the middle of the hall. They stood in front of Ma'at and Osiris, with twenty-one judges on their left and another twenty-one on their right.

The judges were minor deities, each responsible for asking about a single sin. The dead's duty was to deny that they intentionally committed any of the forty-two sins, each sin to its judge. Nevertheless, before this could happen, the dead had to know the names of the forty-two gods. The process is similar to a religious confession, except that it consisted of denying the sins uncommitted rather than reciting the ones committed.

After the confession, the dead were asked to present their heart for weighing against the feather of Ma'at. The ancient Egyptians believed that sin weighed down the heart and soul. In other words, a pure soul's heart should weigh less than the feather of Ma'at, the goddess of order, balance, and truth.

On a golden scale, Osiris took the heart offered to him, and he placed it on one side, then proceeded to place a white feather taken from the wings of Ma'at. If the heart proved heavier than the feather, it was immediately cast down to the ground where the ferocious Ammit devoured it. She was a crocodile-faced demoness with the front half of a lion and the back half of a hippopotamus. After she ate the heart, the soul whom it belonged to disappeared from existence. This permanent death of the soul was an impure heart's punishment.

In the event where the soul's heart proved lighter than the feather, Ma'at would consult with the forty-two judges before the soul was allowed passage into the underworld to walk with Ra through the twelve regions of the Duat. The soul's journey with Ra ended with the Field of Reeds, also known as Aaru. There, where the ground was as fertile and the hunt as bountiful as can be, the pure souls lived and prospered. This was the Egyptians reaching the afterlife, their noblest goal, and one of the things they dedicated their lives to on a daily basis.

The Significance of the Pyramidic Design

While it may seem like a random geometric shape that was simply stable enough to support heavy weights and complex interior designs, the pyramid was much more than that. First of all, the pyramid was believed to be a representation of the Benben, the mound or hill that first sprouted from the primordial waters and started the process of Creation. What supports this theory is the triangular shape of the Benben in ancient Egyptian drawings. Not to mention, the topmost stones that formed the tip of the pyramid were often referred to as the little Benben.

It is also believed that the pyramids represented sun rays descending onto the earth, coinciding with the belief that the souls of the dead often returned to visit the living. The pyramids were considered guiding beacons for the souls in Aaru. They could return to the land of the living, and at the same time, they were seen as a stairway that guides dead souls to the stars, according to the Egyptologist Toby Wilkinson, based in the University of Cambridge.

As for their location, the pyramids were all built on the west bank of the river Nile. It was believed that by placing the pyramids in the west, they would be closer to the underworld since the west is where Ra's solar ship descends into the Duat.

The Contents of a Pyramid

Essentially, the pyramid is a type of tomb, only reserved for kings because the build was quite expensive and required many workers and years of engineering, layering, and design. Inside the pyramids, with respect to their varying size, which depends on the stature of the person who commissioned the build, there are several passages, antechambers, and chambers. While the interior structure may vary, certain architectural and layout elements remain more or less constant.

Canopic Jars

When a person died, it was the priests' duty to mummify and embalm the body before they allowed it to rest. The organs were extracted from the body, except for the heart, which was left in place for the weighing of the heart in the Hall of Ma'at. Then, they were said to be put inside four distinct jars, so they would be reused in case the soul passed the weighing of the heart. The jars were called the canopic jars, and each had a unique lid that bore the head of a god.

The liver was preserved in a jar with a lid shaped like a human head that represented the god Imset. The stomach was preserved under a Jackal-headed lid that belonged to Duamutef, another of Horus's sons. The lungs were protected under the baboon-headed lid of the god Hapi. Lastly, the intestines were stored under the falcon-headed god Qebehsenuef. The four jars were then placed together in a chest or arranged in the burial chamber along with the mummy in its coffin.

Coffin

Naturally, the burial chambers also bore the coffin of the deceased. The coffin's purpose was to preserve the soul's physical body to inhabit it again when its journey through the underworld would be completed. This is why the coffins' lids were often extremely heavy, and the pyramids were heavily sealed and protected by curses against grave robbers.

Funerary Texts

All over the walls of burial rooms, spells, incantations, prayers, and other forms of texts were written for many purposes. First off, it was believed that once the soul awakened after physical death, it was in a state of confusion, struggling to remember who it belonged to and the life it led. Those texts reminded the soul of its life and its deeds, which was essential for it to remember because of the final judgment that awaited.

While for some, the Book of the Dead was written on papyrus and kept safe within the tomb, for others, the instructions for the afterlife were written on tomb walls. These often contained precious information like the names of the assessors of Ma'at and the forty-two sins the soul will have to deny committing. It is worth noting that the forty-two sins differed from one person to another, depending on their occupation and social stature.

There were also instructions on how to get to the underworld, information regarding what happens in the Hall of Ma'at, and the rewards that await. All of that was to prepare the soul and grant it a sense of peace before it was led to stand trial.

Ushabti

These were tiny figures and figurines made of wax, clay, or even marble. Their function was to serve the souls in the afterlife. While the soul enjoyed its time in the Field of Reeds, the figures were meant to come to life, farm, and hunt for the soul of the deceased to have what it desires. It was believed that to distribute the labor among the figures, each figure had to be inscribed with its task.

Sustenance for the Afterlife

It was highly common for the living to leave food, drink, supplies, weapons, jewelry, and even money for the dead to use in the afterlife. It was believed that the dead used the weapons to protect themselves and defeat Ra's enemies as they walked through the horror-filled Duat. They sustained themselves on food and drink before Anubis escorted them to the doors of the Hall of Ma'at and during their journey in the Duat. The rest was said to have been reserved for later use in the afterlife.

The Three Pyramids of Giza

Through the example of the three pyramids, it is apparent how the ancient Egyptian beliefs had an impact on the design of the pyramids. While the evidence is limited due to the passage of grave robbers and occupants who attempted to destroy the structures, the similarities between the inner structures are enough to showcase how dedicated ancient Egyptians were to their concept of death and the afterlife.

The Great Pyramid of Khufu

As the largest of the three, this pyramid was built for King Khufu. It has a descending passage, which turns to an ascending passage, leading to three chambers. The first is called the Grand Gallery; the second is the Queen's Chamber, the third is the King's Chamber. While there is also a great void underneath the pyramid, it isn't physically accessible, which makes it hard to specify whether it serves a purpose or if it simply is an unfinished chamber.

The King's chamber has two shafts, often thought to be air shafts. However, their position, connecting from the burial room to the northern and southern skies, indicates that they are related to the soul's journey from the land of the living. The Queen's Chamber wasn't intended for the queen but for a few of the king's belongings. From what

was discovered, locked behind the room's doors
was a wooden board, a black ball made of stone,
and a copper hook-like tool, all of which are believed to serve a purpose in the king's afterlife as
tools or offerings.

The Pyramid of Khafre

The second-largest pyramid was built for Khafre,
Khufu's son. Inside the burial chamber lies a coffin
made of granite lowered slightly into the ground.
Next to it can be found another pit, believed to
have housed the four canopic jars, but there is no
way of knowing because the grave was not intact
when the excavation parties accessed the room.
Other than the main burial room, another emp-
ty chamber was also discovered, suggesting that
there were offerings left for the reanimated soul of
the dead king.

The Pyramid of Menkaure

King Khafre's successor built the third and small-
est pyramid of the great three for himself. As opposed to the other pyramids, there were two coffins inside the pyramid's burial room. The first

was assumed to belong to the pharaoh himself since it was an 8-foot-long decorated marble sarcophagus. A few wooden parts of the second coffin were found, only remnants, along with the set of bones it housed. Overall, the pyramid is a much more complex structure than the rest, given its symbolism, and seeing as it had three levels with intricately decorated chambers for the dead to rest in peace.

Chapter 5:

Deities and Creatures

Ancient Egyptian mythology abounds with deities and creatures, each with a detailed history, origins, a cult of worshippers, and symbols. The following are only a few of the remarkable gods and monsters found in ancient Egyptian myths.

Thoth

As mentioned previously in Osiris's myth, where he aided Isis and arbitrated between Set and Horus, the god Thoth was best known as the god of wisdom. He was also the scribe of the gods and a personal companion to the great Ra. On many occasions, he is called upon by Ra to fulfill certain duties. And along with Ma'at, he stood by the side of the great god on his journey across the sky and the underworld. In addition, this Ibis-headed god was credited for granting humans the gift of writing. Some accounts also point to him as the reason why calendar years have 365 days instead of 360.

Hapi

The Nile god, mainly linked to the flood that took place each year. While the flood brought destruction to the Nile's structures and homes, it also spewed to the surface the rich soil of the river's bed. Despite the destructive nature of floods, the god was seen as the bearer of fertility and abundance. The god was often depicted with female breasts, which reflected his nurturing nature and a large belly symbolizing the abundance he brings with him.

Bennu

Bennu is a bird made of fire, heavily associated with Ra, the creator god. Some believed that it was a fragment of Ra's soul, and with its cry, it set the process of creation in motion. The bird was also related to a rebirth, linking it to Osiris, and many years later, it was used as a basis for the Grecian legend of the phoenix.

Uraei

These are the cobras of the gods, mostly noticed during Ra's journey through the underworld, where they appear with their many sizes, shapes, and forms. It was believed that a uraeus protected its pharaoh from danger, so pharaohs were often seen wearing the uraeus symbol on their forehead and inside their crowns.

Sekhmet

As narrated early on, she is a lion goddess who almost destroyed humanity when she was ordered to avenge Ra as the human race started conspiring against him. Sekhmet is one of the most feared goddesses in the Egyptian pantheon, and other than the fear-inducing names she was given, like 'mistress of dread,' the literal translation of her name is 'the powerful one.'

Sobek

The crocodile god is different from Ammit, the crocodile-faced monster who devours the hearts of the impure in the Hall of Ma'at. He was associated with the Fayum region in Egypt and mainly served as a protector god to the Egyptians, though he was associated with power, war, and ferocity. Some accounts include him in Osiris's myth as the one who helped Isis gather the dismembered pieces of Osiris. The myth was one of the reasons for his popularity and high stature in the Egyptian pantheon of gods.

Conclusion

After a closer look at ancient Egyptian mythology, it is evident that its creators possessed a great deal of creativity and were fueled by an undying inspiration. They poured their beliefs and everything they had into their stories, which they told on their walls. Even more so, one can see how the elements used in the Egyptian myths have influenced the many civilizations and storytellers that followed.

The ancient Egyptians believed that the world was inactive and in a state of chaos before Ra set the universe in motion. In the Greek creation myths, the world is engulfed in darkness and chaos at first; then, Gaia is born and gives birth to Uranus, the sky, and the other titans who represent the various terrains and elements of our planet. Though Greek mythology takes its liberty when it comes to straying away from its Egyptian counterpart, several elements overlap and remain similar.

Another example is the underworlds of both mythologies. While the Egyptians had the Field of Reeds, the Greeks had the fields of Elysium. Both histories also explain the passage of the sun through the existence of a god who rides a vessel across the sky, Ra and his solar boat, and Apollo and his sun chariot. This is even acknowledged by the Greek poet Herodutus who compares both mythologies and acknowledges their similarities.

Through the gripping themes, such as that of betrayal and revenge, it was also presented in the myths that the Egyptians inspired many stories, including blockbuster Disney movies. In the Lion King (1994), when Scar (Set) plots and kills Mufasa (Osiris), he takes the throne, but then with his reign comes a period of starvation. Who comes to avenge his father and defeat his uncle? None but the one and only Simba (Horus), who regains the throne and restores order in the kingdom.

The same logic could also be applied to the concept of the final judgment and the afterlife. Many cultures and religious traditions have inherited the belief that humans will be judged at the end of their lives, whether by a single ominous deity, forty-two judges, or three kings; the inherent conviction is there in some form or another.

Of course, one could argue that it is human nature to believe in a final judgment and an afterlife. After all, the Egyptians and the Chinese were able to develop the same belief in the concept of balance and order: Ma'at and yin and yang. And while cultures could not have been further apart geographically, they shared a core belief which, in a sense, unified them.

The same could also be said about the common belief in the presence of a soul that resides inside our physical body and then separates from it when we die. Although infinite debates could be spurred about whether the world's mythologies were based on cultural influences or innate human nature, ultimately, one thing becomes clear. Regardless of their origins, these stories are proof that we, as humans, the occupants of this planet earth, share quite a fascinating and unsuspected bond.

References

Budge, E. A. (1904). The Gods of the Egyptians: Studies in Egyptian Mythology (Vol. 1). Methuen & Co.

Hart, G. (2005). The Routledge Dictionary of Egyptian Gods and Goddesses (Second ed.). Routledge.

Plutarch & Fowler, H. N. (1936). Moralia (Vol. 5). Harvard University Press.

Greek and Egyptian Religious Parallels. (n.d.). Www.Saic.Edu. https://www.saic.edu/~lliv-in/research/greeks_egyptian_gods/

Isis and Ra. (n.d.). Www.Ucl.Ac.Uk. Retrieved from https://www.ucl.ac.uk/museums-static/digitalegypt/literature/isisandra.html

Mark, J. J. (2017, April 27). The Negative Confession. Ancient History Encyclopedia; Ancient

History Encyclopedia. https://www.ancient.eu/The_Negative_Confession/

Ra, The Creator God of Ancient Egypt. (2019). Arce.org. https://www.arce.org/resource/ra-creator-god-ancient-egypt

Radford, T., & editor, science. (2001, May 14). Pyramids seen as stairways to heaven. The Guardian. https://www.theguardian.com/world/2001/may/14/humanities.highereducation

Printed in Great Britain
by Amazon